Hello, Little One

A Monarch Butterfly Story

For Zoe Amal, my "little one," and for the monarchs who
demonstrate the strength of nature and the fragility
of life . . . that we find a way to mitigate the damage of
climate change so your existence remains unaltered.
— Z. M. P.

For Essie—because I never would have
done it without you.
— F. H.

Hello, Little One

A Monarch Butterfly Story

Zeena M. Pliska

illustrated by **Fiona Halliday**

PAGE STREET KIDS

Coming out of my egg, I see . . .

green.

I crawl from green leaf
to green leaf.
Eating and waiting.

Waiting for something
other than these green leaves.
Everything is green.

And then I see Orange. Orange is gigantic.
And I am so little.

"Hello?" I call out.

Orange swoops down, down, down.
Graceful and beautiful wings catch the wind.

Then, Orange soars up, up, up, and away.

One day, Orange lands to sip the sweet
nectar from a nearby flower.

I sneak a peek at those magnificent wings.

Our eyes lock and I stop munching.
"Hello, Little One," Orange says.

"Um . . . me? Are you talking to me?" I look down, shyly.

"Yes. I see you watching me every day."

"I love your wings," I say.

"You know, you remind me of me," Orange says.
"Once, I was just like you on this milkweed plant."

"I wish I was like you," I say. "I want to fly over
everything. I want to see everything. I want to know
everything, like you."

"One day you will. For now, enjoy the yummy green
leaves!" And off Orange flies—flit, flutter, and swoop.

"Where are you going?" I call out.

"I'll be back!" Orange responds.

When Orange returns the next day, I show off the interesting lines on my green leaf.

"I remember when everything looked new," Orange says.

Orange shows me how to climb to the very top of the milkweed. "Can you feel the wind push against you, Little One?" Orange asks.

"Is this what flying feels like?"

"Almost," Orange says.

And off Orange flies — flit, flutter, and swoop.
I can't wait to fly with Orange.

"What is the world like?" I ask when Orange returns.
Orange says:

"The sunflowers
are blooming.
So big. So yellow!"

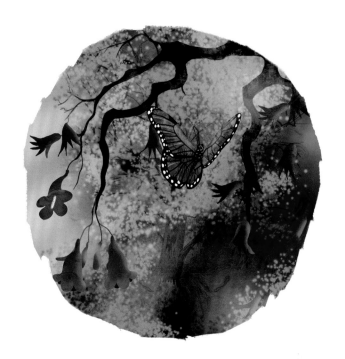

"The jacaranda tree
is bursting purple."

"The bougainvillea
bushes are blossoming
red. Walls of red."

All I've seen are these green leaves.
I can't wait to fly with Orange.

"Where have you been today?"
I ask when Orange lands for a visit.

"I flew above a school today.
The children were laughing and playing."

"I flew through a forest today.
The trees touched the sky."

"I flew over the ocean today.
   The water went on and on forever."

The only place I've been is this milkweed plant.
I can't wait to fly with Orange.

One day Orange says, "You're not so small anymore,
Little One. Your life as a caterpillar is almost complete.
You'll be a chrysalis soon."

"And then I'll be
able to fly?" I ask.

"Not yet. Inside your chrysalis you'll become a butterfly.
Then you will fly!" Orange says.

I dream of how the wind will rush under my wings
when I fly with Orange.

"We'll see so many colors and all the different places,
together," I say.

"My life as a butterfly is almost complete.
 I won't be here when you come out," Orange says.

"Can you wait for me?"

"I don't think so. But you'll see how amazing it is to fly."

"But I want to fly with you," I say.

"I know, but I must go. We all must someday."

"Will you ever come back?" I ask.

"No," Orange says, gently.

We say one last goodbye.

"Your life as a butterfly will be so beautiful," says Orange.
And off Orange flies—flit, flutter, and swoop.

It's time for me to become a chrysalis. In darkness,
I transform. So many changes are happening inside.

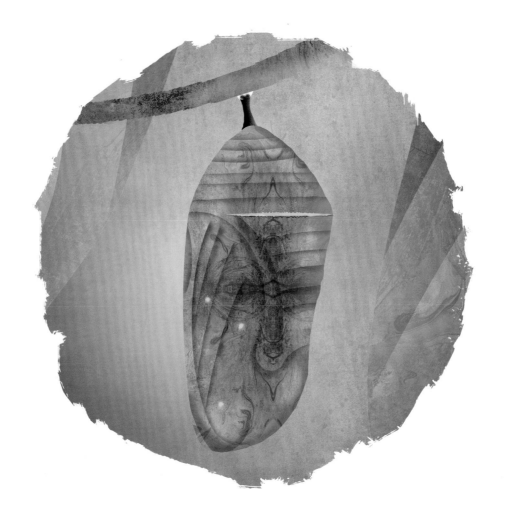

Coming out of my chrysalis,
I look for Orange. I call out.
Nobody answers.

Orange is gone. My own new
orange wings are tiny and
crumpled. I can't fly yet.

Unsteady, unsure, and alone, I wait.
My wings are as wet as tears.

Then, I feel the wind push against me.
I remember Orange and the day I climbed
to the top of the milkweed plant.

Finally, my wings unfold and dry.
They are magnificent.
They catch the wind.

I am graceful and beautiful.
I can flit, flutter, and fly.

I soar high over the world. I see the children playing, and the trees that touch the sky, and the endless ocean.

Then, down below, on my swaying milkweed plant, I see a tiny new caterpillar watching me.

Remembering Orange, I swoop down and land on a nearby flower.

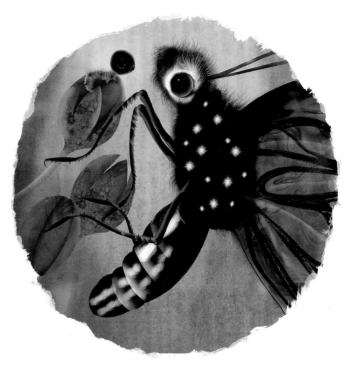

"Hello, little one," I say.

The Life Cycle of a Monarch Butterfly

Egg

Monarch butterflies lay their eggs on milkweed leaves because this is the only plant food the caterpillars eat. The egg takes **3 to 5 days** to hatch.

Larva (Caterpillar)

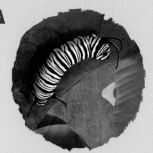

The caterpillar grows and molts (sheds its skin) four times. The time between each molt is called an instar. Through the five instars, its appearance changes slightly. It devours milkweed until it is two inches long. The monarch is a caterpillar for **9 to 14 days**.

Adult (Butterfly)

If the monarch emerges as a butterfly in spring or early summer, it will live for **2 to 5 weeks**. However, if it is part of the generation that emerges in the late summer or early fall, it can live up to **9 months**. This generation migrates over 2,000 miles south for the winter before returning to its breeding grounds.

Pupa (Chrysalis)

Next, the caterpillar spins a silk mat and hangs upside down in a J-shape. Its skin splits open a fifth and final time, and underneath is a chrysalis. Inside the chrysalis, the caterpillar's body reorders into a butterfly in a process called *metamorphosis*. This takes **8 to 15 days**.

Bibliography

Merlin, Christine, Robert J. Gegear, and Steven M. Reppert. "Monarch Butterfly Migration." *AccessScience* (2011). https://doi.org/10.1036/1097-8542.YB110062

"Monarch Biology." MonarchNet. Accessed August 20, 2019. https://www.monarchnet.org

Pringle, Laurence. *An Extraordinary Life: The Story of a Monarch Butterfly.* New York: Orchard Books, 1997.

"Rearing Monarchs: Overview." MonarchWatch. Accessed August 20, 2019. https://www.monarchwatch.org/rear/

University of Minnesota. "Monarch Life Cycle." Monarch Lab. Accessed August 20, 2019. https://monarchlab.org/biology-and-research/biology-and-natural-history/breeding-life-cycle/life-cycle/